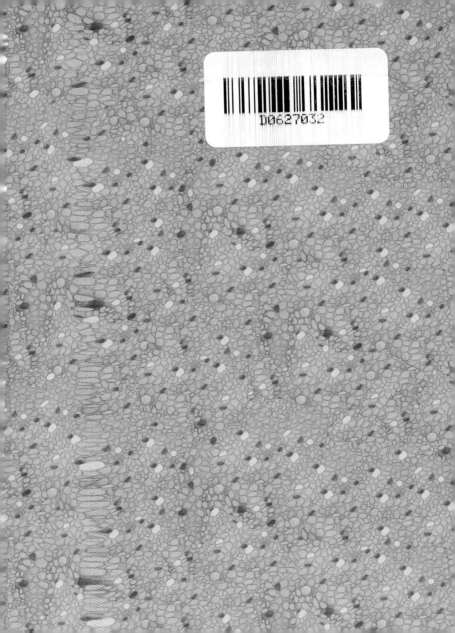

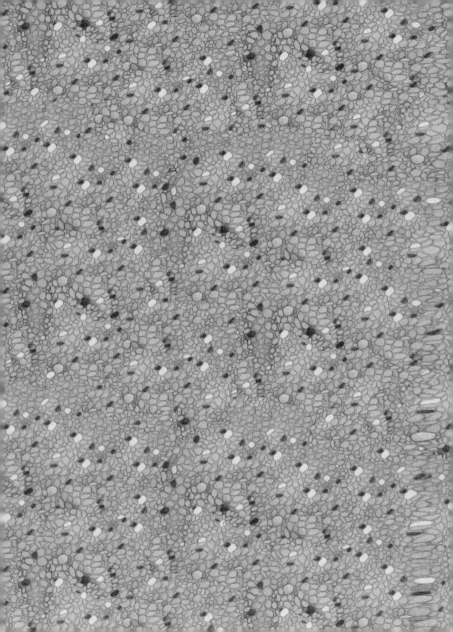

The Moonshine Dragon

Cornelia Funke

With illustrations by

Mónica Armiño

Barrington Stoke

First published in Great Britain in 2014 by
Barrington Stoke Ltd
18 Walker Street, Edinburgh, EH3 7LP

www.barringtonstoke.co.uk

This edition first published 2016
Reprinted 2018

Title of the original German edition:
Lesepiraten Champion – Der Mondscheindrache
© 2011 Loewe Verlag GmbH, Bindlach

Illustrations © 2016 Mónica Armiño
Translation © 2014 Barrington Stoke

A CIP catalogue record for this book is available
from the British Library upon request

ISBN: 978-1-78112-603-5

Printed in China by Leo

This book is super readable for young readers beginning
their independent reading journey.

1046689

For Robin

CONTENTS

Chapter 1

A Dragon
and a Knight

The moon shone into Patrick's room. It turned the carpet silver. Even Patrick's jeans on the chair looked as if they were woven out of silver threads.

Who could sleep on a night like this?

Patrick lay in his bed, stared out of the window and counted the stars.

Patrick had almost dropped off to sleep when he was startled by a soft rustling sound on the floor by his bed.

He peered down to see what it was.

There was a book on the floor.
Patrick had read the book earlier that
day. It was about dragons and knights.
Now it lay open on the carpet, even
though Patrick was sure he had closed it.

Strange.

Patrick reached down to close the book. Then he heard another sound. The white pages moved, as if an invisible hand had turned them over.

Then Patrick heard a soft snort. He was so startled that he hid under his blankets. After a moment, he peeped out and looked down at the book.

Now Patrick could hear a loud panting noise. As he watched, a scaly tail appeared from between the pages of the book. The tail was followed by two claws, then a silver body with wings and spikes on its back and then – THUD! A dragon slid out from the book and landed on Patrick's carpet.

"Oh dear, oh dear!" the dragon moaned. He looked around. "Where am I? I was in my den. Where have I ended up now?"

The dragon was very beautiful to look at. He had silver and blue scales and a great long tail. He was just like

the picture Patrick had always had in his mind of how a dragon would look. The only difference was that this dragon would fit inside a jam jar.

The pages of the book moved again, and this time Patrick heard the clatter of hooves and the clink of iron.

"He's coming!" the dragon whispered in horror. "He's following me. He's found me! I have to hide. But where? Where?"

The dragon twisted his long neck this way and that. In the end he spotted Patrick's toy castle, in the darkest corner of the room.

"Yes!" he cried. "That's perfect!"

The dragon spread his silver wings as if he wanted to fly, but it seemed he couldn't manage more than a tired flutter.

"Well then, I shall just have to run," he said.

The dragon ran across the moonlit carpet to the castle, as fast as his legs could carry him.

The dragon was only a human-sized step away from the book when a horse sprang out of it. On the horse's back was a knight in armour with a plume of white feathers on his helmet. The horse reared up and the knight looked around.

Patrick ducked ever deeper under his blankets.

"Ha! I will get you, you evil fire-worm!" the knight roared when he spotted the dragon. "This time you will not escape!"

The knight galloped up to the dragon with his sword held high.

"Stop!" Patrick yelled. He pushed
his blankets off and jumped out of bed.
"Leave the dragon alone, OK?" he said to
the knight.

"Whoa!" the little knight cried and his horse stopped. The knight stared up at Patrick. The dragon looked too – at Patrick, the knight and the horse. He let out a cry of alarm and then disappeared into the toy castle.

"A giant!" the knight cried. "By God, we are in a land of giants!"

"Nonsense!" Patrick said. He leaned down to talk to the knight. "You're in my room and no dragons are hunted here. Is that clear?"

"Peace, hideous giant!" the knight roared. "The White Knight is not afraid of you!" He waved his lance, spurred his horse and galloped straight for Patrick's bare legs.

"Hey, stop that!" Patrick cried. "Put away that spear!"

But the knight had already poked his tiny spear into Patrick's shin.

"Ow!" Patrick cried. "Are you crazy?"

Patrick was furious. He snatched at the knight and lifted him off his horse.

And that's when it happened.

As soon as Patrick touched the knight, he began to shrink. Down, down, down he shrank – and fast! Patrick only just managed to pull the knight off his horse.

A few seconds later, he was down beside him on the carpet – and Patrick was even shorter than the knight!

The White Knight was the first to recover from the shock.

He jumped to his feet and drew
his sword. Clink, clink, clink went his
armour.

"Aha!" he growled. "You are a
wizard, a vile enchanter."

"What nonsense!" Patrick cried. He got to his feet.

"Liar!" the knight yelled. "Slimy devilish warlock!"

He lunged this way and that as he attacked Patrick with his sword.

Patrick had to make a wild leap to one side to stop his head being cut off. Then he ran. He ran towards the castle, faster than he had ever run before.

Patrick was in luck. The White Knight's armour was so heavy that he struggled to get back on his horse.

When at last he made it back into the saddle, Patrick was almost at the castle gate. But two crayons and a rubber were lying on the carpet, blocking his way.

Patrick struggled to climb over the crayons as the knight galloped closer and closer.

'Oh no!' Patrick thought. 'If only I'd listened to Mum when she told me to keep my room tidy.'

Patrick used all his strength to lift himself over the crayons and reach the drawbridge of the castle.

He stumbled inside and grabbed the handle that cranked up the bridge to close it. His arms shook as he turned the handle.

With a creak, the bridge began to lift. At the very last second it slammed shut and closed the castle door. Phew!

When he saw this, the angry White Knight beat his shield on the castle wall. It made a sound like thunder.

Chapter 2

A Good Plan

"Oh man!" Patrick groaned. His legs trembled and he leaned against the inside wall of the castle.

"Are you really a wizard?" a voice behind Patrick asked.

Patrick spun round. The dragon! He had forgotten about the dragon. It was crouched in the far corner of the castle yard.

"I'm not a wizard," Patrick said. "And I'm not a giant. I'm just a normal boy."

"You would say that," the dragon said. "But the boys I know are not as big as castle towers. And they do not change size all of a sudden."

"I've never changed size before," Patrick told him. "I have no idea how that happened."

"Must be moonlight magic," the dragon said. "I've heard of such a thing before. When the moonlight disappears, the magic disappears too."

"I'm glad to hear it!" Patrick said. "It's pretty dangerous to be so small! Can you see what that stupid bucket-head is doing out there?"

The dragon stretched his long neck, but the castle wall was too high for him to see over.

Patrick climbed the stairs that led to the top of the wall, and peered over the battlements.

"I see him," he whispered. "He has got off his horse and now he is looking at my toys. What's he up to?"

"Oh, he'll be looking for treasure," the dragon said. "If the White Knight isn't collecting dragon heads, then he's hunting for treasure."

"Well, he'll have his work cut out for him finding treasure in my bedroom," Patrick said.

"Maybe so, but he's still going to get us," the dragon wailed.

"Nonsense!" said Patrick.

"Don't be so sure. The White Knight is stronger and braver than you think!" the dragon said.

"He has killed more dragons and knights than anyone can count," the dragon went on. "So far I've always managed to escape, but now ..." He shook his beautiful head. "Now it seems I must die in this strange world, where I've only just arrived."

Patrick came back down the stairs. "You crawled out of a book," he told the dragon.

The dragon looked at him in surprise. "What book?" he asked.

"One with lots of stories in it about dragons," said Patrick.

"I'm not from a story!" the dragon said in a huff.

"You are so," Patrick said. "Anyway, why can't you fly?"

"The White Knight has chased me for so long and so far that I've not had time to eat," the dragon said. "A dragon cannot fly on an empty stomach. Perhaps if you gave me something to eat –"

The dragon stopped and his ears pricked up. "I think the knight's coming back!" he whispered.

Patrick scrambled to climb back up the steps to the top of the wall.

The White Knight was now heading for the castle at full gallop. He no longer held his lance in his hands. Instead, he held a crayon. There was a terrible crash as he rammed the crayon against the closed drawbridge. The plastic drawbridge shattered like a broken eggshell and a hole appeared in the middle. The White Knight laughed. He threw the broken crayon on the carpet and picked up a new one.

"Oh, no!" Patrick groaned. "The bridge didn't hold out for very long."

Patrick scanned the room in the hope he might spot something they could use

to stop the knight. The plastic lances from his toy knight would be no use. .Then he saw the big digger he had got for his last birthday. It was made of metal and it worked by remote control.

'Where did I put the remote control?' Patrick thought. His eyes fell on the bookshelf. Of course – there was the control, on the third shelf from the top. There was no way someone as small as him could get up there.

The White Knight rammed the bridge a second time. The hole he had made in the plastic was getting bigger.

And then Patrick had an idea.

"Hey, you!" he called down to the dragon. "Do you eat bread?"

"I'll eat anything!" the dragon called back.

Patrick ran to the tall castle tower. It looked very high and there were no stairs. But, at the top of the tower, there were pellets of bread that Patrick had made to fire from the castle's big cannon.

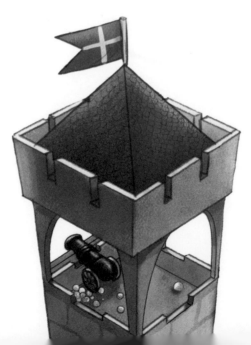

Patrick's fingers trembled as he pulled himself up the castle wall. Higher and higher he climbed. The knight pulled on his horse's reins to hold it still, and he watched Patrick climb.

With his very last bit of strength, Patrick pulled himself over the battlements of the tower and flopped onto the platform at the top. The bread pellets were there – some were dried-up, but most of them were all right.

"Catch!" Patrick shouted to the dragon.

The dragon opened his mouth and swallowed one pellet after another.

Chapter 3

The Iron Dragon

The White Knight and his horse stormed the drawbridge again. Now it hung all crooked on the thin chain that attached it to the castle.

"S-s-s-s-s!" the dragon hissed as the last pellet of bread vanished into his belly. He licked his lips. Then he beat his powerful wings and flew up to Patrick on the castle tower.

"Miserable fire-worm!" the White Knight roared from below. "That will not save you and the wizard."

The dragon stuck out his tongue in reply.

"Where should I go?" he asked Patrick.

Patrick pointed to the bookshelf.

"Get on," said the dragon.

Patrick clambered onto the dragon's back and held onto his big spikes.

"Hold on!" the dragon called, and he spiralled up into the air.

The White Knight brandished his
sword and cursed. But Patrick laughed.
It was wonderful, flying on the dragon's

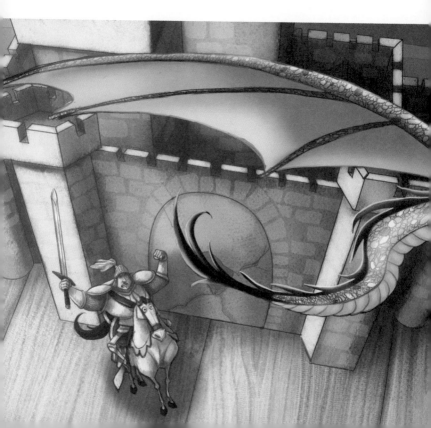

back. His room looked like a strange
landscape below them as they flew
across it in the moonlight.

The dragon rose higher and higher and landed on the shelf right next to the remote control.

"How was that?" he asked, as he folded his silver wings back together again.

"It was wonderful!" Patrick said.
"And now, watch this! We'll scare that
stupid knight back into his book."

Patrick and the dragon were both
so small that it was not easy for them
to point the huge remote control at the
giant digger, but together they managed
it.

"Let's go," Patrick whispered.

Patrick used his little hands to turn the switch and then moved the knob that steered the digger.

The digger began to jolt over the carpet. Straight towards the knight.

The knight's horse reared up when it saw the bucket of the giant digger coming towards it.

"Ha, a pathetic Iron Dragon!" the White Knight roared. "Attack!"

The knight spurred his horse on to attack, but it went wild. It reared and bucked and lashed out with its hooves until it threw the knight off its back. And then the horse galloped back to the book and, with one big leap, it disappeared between the pages.

The White Knight scrambled to his feet. With a bellow of rage, he charged at the digger.

"He's mad!" Patrick said. He pressed the button to lower the digger bucket, and the bucket scooped the knight up off the carpet. The knight kicked and screamed. He waved his sword at the digger, but he was trapped in the bucket.

Patrick used the remote control to drive the digger straight at the book. "Off you go!" he shouted. "And don't come back!"

Then he shovelled the White Knight back into the book. The knight slipped between the pages and was gone.

"Thank goodness!" the dragon said. "He's gone! But what are you going to do with the Iron Dragon now?"

"I'm going to switch the Iron Dragon off," Patrick said.

"So you are a wizard!" the dragon cried.

"No, I'm not," Patrick told him.
"Can you fly me down to the floor now,
please?"

Patrick got up onto the dragon's back
and off they flew.

Chapter 4

Moonlight Magic

The dragon flew over the room and set Patrick down on his bed.

"What are you going to do now?" Patrick asked the dragon. "You can't go back to your story. That mad knight is there."

The dragon shrugged. "Where else can I go?"

"You could stay with me," Patrick said.

"You are very kind," the dragon said. "But I would rather go back to my own world."

"I've got it!" Patrick cried. "Why don't you go to another story? There are stories in my book with dragons and no knights."

"Really?" the dragon said, his eyes wide open.

"I promise," Patrick said. "Hold on."

Patrick slid down the bed sheets and ran over to the book. It seemed so huge now he was so small. He turned the big, heavy pages of the book.

"Yes, here," he said. "Page 123. This is the place for you."

"If you say so ..." The dragon flapped his wings over the open page. "OK! Say goodbye. I'm going into this new story now ..."

Then – whoosh! The dragon vanished in between the pages of the book.

"Thank you!" Patrick heard him call, from far, far away.

Then Patrick was alone again in his room. The moon still shone through the window.

Patrick yawned as he climbed back into his bed. He curled up on the pillow and covered himself with a corner of the blanket.

"Moonlight magic," he murmured. "Well, let's see."

When Patrick woke up the next morning, he was as big as ever. The same size as a normal boy. But the broken castle and the broken crayons proved that last night's adventure had not been a dream.

From then on, every moonlit night, Patrick left an open book next to his bed.

But as for the pages which told the story of the White Knight ... Patrick stuck those pages firmly together.

Our books are tested
for children and young people by
children and young people.

Thanks to everyone who consulted on
a manuscript for their time and effort in
helping us to make our books better
for our readers.